BEHIND MR. BUNYAN

A true story

by Agnes Beaumont

Grace & Truth Books

Sand Springs, Oklahoma

ISBN # 1-58339-133-9
First printings, 1700's (date unknown)
Printed by Triangle Press, 1996
Current printing, Grace & Truth Books, 2002

Cover design by Ben Gundersen

Grace & Truth Books
3406 Summit Boulevard
Sand Springs, Oklahoma   74063
Phone: 918 245 1500

www.graceandtruthbooks.com
email: gtbooksorders@cs.com

TABLE OF CONTENTS

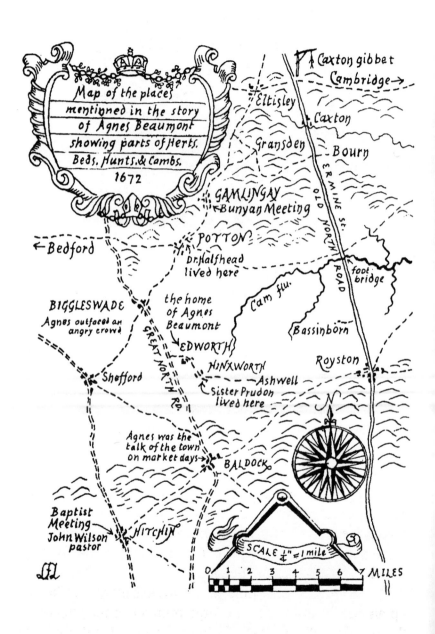

Map of the places
mentioned in the story
of Agnes Beaumont
showing parts of Herts.
Beds, Hunts. & Cambs.
1672

Caxton gibbet
Cambridge →

Eltisley

Caxton

Gransden

Bourn

GAMLINGAY
Bunyan Meeting

POTTON

Dr. Halfhead
lived here

← Bedford

foot
bridge

Cam flu.

BIGGLESWADE
Agnes outfaced an
angry crowd

the home
of Agnes
Beaumont

Bassinborn

EDWORTH

HINXWORTH

Royston

Ashwell

Sister Prudon
lived here

Shefford

Agnes was the
talk of the town
on market days →

BALDOCK

Baptist
Meeting
John Wilson
pastor

HITCHIN

N

OLD NORTH ROAD

ERMINE ST.

GREAT NORTH RD.

SCALE ¼" = 1 mile

0 1 2 3 4 5 6 7 MILES

BEHIND MR. BUNYAN

My name is Agnes Beaumont and I was born at Edworth, about nine miles from Hitchin, in the year 1650. At the time of the happenings which I am about to relate, I was twenty-four years of age, and kept house for my widowed father. My brother John was married and lived at another farmhouse close to ours.

Although I was only young, I had lived through many changes in the affairs of the country. I can remember as a child hearing of the death during a great September storm of Lord Protector Cromwell. Later on there were bonfires and ringing of church bells for the new King—Charles the Second.

Ever since the time of Cromwell there had been, up and down the country, a large number of meetings for the worship of God, especially in those midland parts of

England. This was not allowed by the government, and there was much persecution of those who would not give it up. There were several meetings round about us. At Gamlingay there was one, and another at Hitchin where John Wilson was pastor, while at Bedford, Mr. Bunyan was in charge.

When I was not much more than twenty years old, my father, my brother and I began to go to the Bedford Meeting. Oh, how we did feel our hearts stirred by the wonderful preaching of that godly Mr. Bunyan! who, for the best part of twelve years, had lain in Bedford jail for his faith. We heard him with profit to our souls. I was so full of joy, that it was as if I had been in heaven. There was scarce a corner in the house or barns, stable

or cowhouses, under the hedges or in the wood where I did not pour out my soul to God. This often made me cry so that some would say, "Agnes, why do you grieve and go crying thus?," while all the time my tears were for joy and love of Jesus Christ.

Nothing would content me but I must be joined with Mr. Bunyan and his people of the church. This was not so easily done then as it is nowadays. In those days, everyone that would be a member had to give an account before the congregation of what God had done for them, in saving them from sin and bringing them effectively to Christ. If anything about this matter was not clear, their application to join the church was refused, or they were told to wait for a time until it was clear.

But in the end of 1672 I was received into fellowship with four others, and Mr. Bunyan wrote our names in the book. Indeed, he had but then begun to keep the church book himself, and mine was the first name that he wrote therein with his own hand.

My brother John was just as full of these things as myself. He did not join our meeting, but was like to have been in trouble. He was constable at Edworth and was warned for not going to the parish church. However, nothing more came of it and he and his wife were at meetings as often as I was.

With my dear father, alas, it was different. There were many in those days who spread the most wicked slander about us, especially about Mr. Bunyan. It began to be rumoured, up and down among the people, that he

was a witch, a Jesuit, or a highwayman. Foremost among those who spread these lies was our own priest, Mr. Lane, who even said that Mr. Bunyan had his misses and two wives, with much more of the same sort as you will see hereafter. These lying tales made us that knew the man laugh even to think of such things being said against him. But my father, like many others, gave heed to them and grew afterwards as hot against the

meetings and against Mr. Bunyan as he had been formerly in favour of them.

I must also mention in this place another who was an enemy to the godly, and that was Mr. Freery, our lawyer. Some time before this he had helped my father to draw up his will, in the which he persuaded him to leave everything in my favour. Mr. Freery hoped to marry me for my portion. When I began to be taken up with my new friends at the meeting, I soon found he had little patience for that sort of thing. In short, he was another who, though friendly at first, grew afterwards to be my enemy on account of the meetings.

Before God brought that trial upon me of which I am now to write, I had many Scriptures run into my mind. Wherever I was, this verse would often dart into my mind: "And call upon me in the day of trouble: I will deliver thee, and thou shalt glorify Me." Thought I, "this must point at something to come, for now I have more comfort than trouble." And that other Scripture would come to me: "When thou goest through the fire I will be with thee, and through the waters they shall not overflow thee." Many such Scriptures I saw had bitter and sweet in them. Often I said to my dear friend Sister Prudon, "I have some heavy thing coming upon me, but I know not what it will be."

Many dreams I had which were, some of them, I believe from God. I often dreamed I was like to lose my life and could hardly escape with it. Sometimes I thought that men ran after me, and sometimes that I was tried before a judge and jury, and methought I did escape and that was all.

One dream I told Sister Prudon which she reminded me of after my father was dead. Methought that in my father's yard grew an old apple tree and it was full of fruit. Then one night, about the middle of the night, there came a very sudden storm of wind and blew this tree up by the roots. I was sorely troubled to see it so suddenly blown down.

I ran to it, as it lay upon the ground, to lift it up to have it grow in its place again. I thought I saw it turned up by the roots, and I stood lifting at it as long as I had any strength, first with one arm, then the other, but could not stir it out of its place. At last I left it and ran to my brother to call for help. And when my brother and his men did come they could not make this tree grow in his place again. Oh, how troubled I was for this tree!

Soon afterwards there was to be a meeting at Gamlingay. For about a week beforehand I was much in prayer for two things. One was that God would be pleased to make my father willing. Sometimes he was

against my going and in those days it was like death to me, to be kept from the meetings. I had found by experience that the only way to prevail with my father was to pray hard to God beforehand to make him willing, and had often found success according as I had

cried to God. When I prayed hard I found my father willing and when I prayed less I found him more difficult.

The other thing which I was begging of the Lord was that He would be pleased to give me His presence at His Table and that I might have such a sight of my dying Saviour that it might melt my heart. In those days I was always laying up many a prayer in heaven against the time I came to the Lord's Table.

Well, it did please the Lord to grant me these two things. The day before the meeting I asked my father to let me go to it, and he seemed not very willing. But I pleaded with him, telling him that I would do what I had to do in the morning before I went, and that I would come home again at night. At last he was willing. So, on Friday morning, which was the day of the meeting, I made ready to go. My father asked who was taking me. I said I thought it would be Mr. Wilson who was calling at my brother's house that morning on the way, as had been already arranged between them at Hitchin market on the Tuesday beforehand. My father said nothing.

So, when I was ready, I went to my brother expecting to meet Mr. Wilson and ride behind him on horseback.

There I waited, and nobody came. At last my heart began to ache and I fell, a-crying for fear I should not be able to go. For my brother had told me he could not let me have a horse because they were all at work, and that his wife was to ride behind him so that in no way could he help me. It was the depth of winter so I could not go on foot.

Now I was afraid my prayers were all lost. Thought I, "I prayed to God to make my father willing to let me go, and that I might have the presence of God in that meeting, but my way is hedged up with thorns." There I waited and looked many a long look.

"Mr. Wilson said he would come this way," said my brother, but he did not come. Oh, thought I, that God would be pleased to put it into the heart of someone to come this way and to make some way or other for me to go! Still I waited with my heart full of fears.

Behind Mr. Bunyan

At last, unexpectedly, came Mr. Bunyan and called on my brother on his way to the meeting. But the sight of him caused both sorrow and joy in me. I was glad to see him but I was also afraid, because I thought he would not carry me to the meeting behind him, and how to ask him I did not know, for fear he should deny me. So I got my brother to ask him.

"I must desire you," said he to Mr. Bunyan, "to carry my sister behind you." "No!" answered he, "I will not carry her." These were cutting words to me and made me weep bitterly. My brother asked him again.

"If you do not carry her it will break her heart." He replied with the same words, and then, turning to me, he said, "Your father would be grievously angry with me."

"If you please to carry me," said I, "I will venture that." At last, with many entreaties, my brother

10

persuaded him, and I climbed up behind. Oh, how glad I was to be going.

I heard afterwards that almost before we had ridden out of the yard my father came to speak with some of the farmhands, and asked who it was that I was riding behind. When they told him it was Mr. Bunyan, he flew into a passion and ran down to the end of the close, thinking to have met us in the fields and intending to pull me off the back of the horse, so angry was he. But we had gone by first.

We had not gone far before my heart was puffed up. I began to have high thoughts of myself, and was proud to think I should ride behind such a man as he was, and was glad when anybody saw us as we rode alone. Sometimes he would speak to me about the things of heaven. Indeed, I thought myself a happy lady that day, first because that it had pleased God to make a way for me to go to the meeting, and secondly because I had the honour to ride behind Mr. Bunyan. But, as you shall hear, my pride had a fall.

Coming to the town end, there met us a priest, one Mr. Lane who lived, as I remember at Bedford but used to preach at Edworth. He knew us both, and spoke to us and gazed after us as we rode along, as if he would have stared his eyes out. Afterwards he made scandal about us in a very base manner and did raise a very wicked report of us, which was altogether false, blessed be God.

So we came to Gamlingay. After a while the meeting began and God made it a blessed meeting to me indeed! When I was at the Lord's Table my soul was filled with consolation. I found such a return of prayer that I was scarcely able to bear up under it. Oh, I had such a sight of Jesus Christ, it broke my heart to pieces.

The Bunyan Meeting House. Gamlingay   *LH 30.12.'62*

I longed to be with Him and fain would have died in the place if I might have gone straight to Him. I have often thought since of the goodness and grace of the Lord Jesus, that He should so visit my soul on that day.

WET AND MUDDY!

The Lord Jesus knew what trials and temptations I had to meet with that night and for the next few days. Oh, what pity He had towards me in showing me His love on that very day.

Well, when the meeting was done, I began to think how I should get home. Though Mr. Bunyan came from Edworth he was not going back that way. It was almost night and very muddy, and I had promised my father to come home by nightfall. My thoughts began to work and my heart to be full of fears lest I should not get home that night. Just as it had cost me a lot of trouble to get to the meeting, so it cost me even more to get home again, but, blessed be God, during the meeting all such matters were kept out of my thoughts. So I went, first to one, and then to another asking if there was anyone who could at least carry me some part of the way home. There was only one who could help me and that was a maid that lived at Hinksworth, half a mile from my father's house. The roads were so muddy and deep that I was afraid to ride behind her. But in the end I ventured and she put me down at Sister Prudon's gate.

So I came ploshing home with mud over my shoes, having no pattens on. I made what haste I could, hoping I should be at home before my father was a-bed, but when I came to the house I saw no light in it. So I went to the door and found it locked, with the key in it. Then my heart began to ache with fear, for when I had been out late at other times and if my father happened to go to bed before I came home, he would take the key to bed with him and hand it to me through the window. However, I went to his window and called to him. He asked who was there.

"It is me, father," said I, "pray will you let me in, I am come home wet and muddy."

THE NIGHT IS LONG AND COLD

"Where you have been all day, go at night,"
replied he, with many other such things. He was very
angry with me for riding behind Mr. Bunyan and said I
should never come within his doors again except I would
leave going after that man; for some enemies in the town
had set my father against him by false reports which they
affirmed were true, and my father, poor man, believed
them.

So I stood at his window pleading and entreating
with him, begging and crying to him to let me in. But all
in vain! For instead of letting me in, he bid me begone
from the window, or else he would get up and throw me
out of the yard. I stood awhile at the window silent. A
thought came to me, "How if I should come at last when
the door is shut and Jesus Christ should say to me
'Depart from me, I know you not.'?" Then it came
secretly into my mind, that seeing my father would not
let me come in, I would spend the night in prayer. "Oh,"
thought I, "so I will, I will go into the barn and spend
this night in prayer to God, that Jesus Christ will not shut
me out at last." But this thought immediately darted in,
"No, go to your brother's house. There you may have a
warm bed and the night is long and cold." These and

many frightful thoughts came to mind. How did I know but that I might be knocked on the head in the barn before morning, or if not so, I might catch my death of cold.

At last I began to comply with these fears. Thought I, "It may be so indeed, this being a lone house and none near it, and it is a very cold night, I shall never be able to abide in the barn until morning." Then one Scripture after another came into my mind, such as that word, "Pray to thy Father that seeth in secret and thy Father that seeth thee in secret shall reward thee openly;" and that verse, "Call upon Me and I will answer thee, and show thee great and mighty things, that thou knewest not;" also many a good word beside that I have forgotten. I thought I had need go and pray to my Heavenly Father indeed.

KEEP SCARES OUT OF MY HEART

Into the barn I went and it was a very dark night. I found I was again attacked by Satan, but having received some strength from God and His Word, I spoke out with these and such like words, "Satan, my Father hath thee on a chain. Thou canst not hurt me." So I went to prayer. Indeed it was a blessed night to me, a night to be remembered to my life's end. A night of prayer and a night of praise. The Lord was pleased to keep scares out of my heart all the night after. It froze vehemently but I felt no cold. The mud was frozen on my shoes by morning.

As I was in prayer, that Scripture came with mighty power: "Beloved, think it not strange concerning the fiery trials that are to try you." That word "beloved" made music in my heart, yet the other part of the words had dread in it—"think it not strange concerning the fiery trials that are to try you." I saw that my father shutting me out of doors was a great trial. I thought, what could be worse to me than that. Still the same Scripture would run through and through my heart, yet that first word, "beloved," sounded louder to me than all the rest. I saw the verse had got bitter and sweet in it, but that it was my mercy to be the beloved of God. So I prayed that He would stand by me and strengthen me, whatever I had to meet with.

One time in the night I was a little cast down. Grief began to seize upon me, to think that I should lose my father's love for going to seek after Jesus Christ. I went to prayer again and was bewailing the loss of my father's love and saying, "Lord, what will become of me if I should fail of Thy love too?," when that good word darted into my mind, "The Father Himself loveth you." "Oh, blessed be God," said I, "that is enough, do with me what seems good in Thy sight."

The morning came on. When it was light I peeped through the cracks of the barn door to see when my father would come out of the house. At last he unlocked the door and came out. Then he locked the door after him and put the key in his pocket. This looks very bad for me, thought I, for I knew by that he was still resolved I should not go in, though he did not know I was so near as I was. That good word—"Beloved, think it not strange concerning the fiery trials that are to try you," still sounded in my heart.

So my father came into the barn where I was with his pitchfork in his hand to serve the cows. When he opened the door he was astounded to see me there with my riding clothes still on. I suppose he thought I had gone to my brother's house.

"Good morrow, father," said I to him. "I have had a cold night's lodging here, but God hath been good to me or else I should have had a worse." He said it was no matter. I prayed him to let me go in. "I hope, father," said I, "you are not angry with me still." I followed him about the yard as he went to feed the cows but he would not hear me. The more I entreated him, the more angry he was with me, and said I should never come within his door again unless I would promise him never to go to a meeting again as long as he lived.

"Father," said I, "my soul is worth more than that. If you could stand in my stead before God to give an account for me at the great day, then I would obey you in this as in other things." But all that I could say prevailed nothing with him.

At last some of my brother's men came into the yard for something he had sent them for. When they went back they told my brother that I was shut out of doors. "For she," said they, "hath her riding clothes on still."

My brother was troubled to hear this and came in haste to my father. He did what he could to persuade him to be reconciled to me and to let me in, but father was more passionate with my brother than with me and would not hear him. So my brother came to me and said, "Come, child, go home with me, thou wilt catch thy death with the cold." But I bid him go home alone, for I saw that my father was more provoked with what he said than he was with me, though my brother spoke very mildly to him. I had a mind to stay a little longer to see what I could do with my father.

I followed him about the yard and sometimes got hold of his arms and cried and hung about him, saying, "Pray, father, let me go in." Afterwards I wondered at my own daring, he being such a hasty man that many times when he hath been angry, I have been glad to get me out of his presence, though once his anger was over, he was as good-natured a man as lived.

When I saw that I could not prevail with him, I went and sat down by the door. He walked about the yard with the key in his pocket and would not come near the house as long as I was there. After I had sat there for some time I began to feel faint because of the cold, for it was a very sharp morning and it grieved me to be the occasion of my father staying out in the cold so long, for I saw he would not go in as long as I was there.

I'LL THROW YOU INTO THE POND!

So I went to my brother's house. They gave me something to refresh me. As soon as I was warm I desired to retire and be alone and went up to one of my sister's rooms to pray, for the more I met with, the more I cried to the Lord.

About the middle of the day, which was Saturday, I said to my sister, "Will you go with me to my father to see what he will say to me now?" When we came to the door we found it locked and my father in the house; for he would not go out, but he would lock the door and put the key in his pocket. Neither would he go into the house but he would lock the door after him.

We went to the window, and my sister said, "Father, where are you?" He came to the window. "Father," said my sister, "I hope your anger is over and that you will let Agnes come in." I also prayed him to be reconciled to me and fell a-crying very much, for indeed at that time my heart was full of grief and sorrow to see my father so angry with me still, and to hear what he said, which now I shall not mention, except this one thing—that he would never give me a penny as long as he lived; nor when he died, but would leave his money to strangers.

Now to tell the truth, these were very hard sayings to me, and at the hearing of them my heart began to sink. Thought I to myself, "What will become of me? To go to service and work for my living is a new thing to me, so young as I am too. What shall I do?" Then this thought came into my mind. "Well, I have a good God to go to still," and that word did comfort me: "For my father and my mother have forsaken me, but the Lord will take me up." So my sister stood pleading with him, but all in vain. Then I asked him that as he did not please to let me come in, to give me my Bible and pattens. But he would not, and said again that he was resolved I should never have one penny, nor pennyworth, as long as he lived; nor when he died.

As I said, I was very much cast down at this. Now did my thoughts begin to work. Thought I, "What shall I do? I am now in a miserable case." I went home with my sister again crying bitterly. Indeed unbelief and carnal reasoning now got in at a great rate, notwithstanding God had been so wonderfully good to me last night in the barn.

At night I had a mind to go again to my father, "But," thought I, "I will go alone;" for I saw he was more angry with my brother that morning and with my sister at noon than he was with me, "And," thought I, "now he hath been alone one night, and hath nobody to do anything for him, it may be he will let me come in." I considered which way to go. "I will go," thought I, "by such a byway that he shall not see me till I come to the door. If I find it open I will go in. He will think I will come no more tonight, and so it may be the door will be open. If it is, I will go in, let my father do with me what he pleases. If he doth throw me out, he does; I will venture!"

So I went. When I came to the door it stood ajar with the key on the outside and my father in the house. I pushed the door softly to go in. But my father was a-coming through the passage to come out. He saw me coming in and ran hastily to the door and slammed it. If I had not been very quick one of my legs would have been trapped between the door and the threshold. He had shut the door. The key was on the outside for he had no time to take the key out, but bolted the door from within. I would not be so uncivil as to lock my father in, but I took the key out of the door and put it into my pocket. "It may be," thought I, "that presently my father will come out to feed the cows," for I saw they were not served up for the night. "I will go stand behind the house, and when I hear him come out I will go in. When I am in I will rely on his mercy." I stood listening. After a while I heard him come out, but before he went up the yard to serve the cows he came and looked behind the house. There he saw me stand. Now, behind the house was a pond and only a narrow path between the house and the pond. There I stood close up to the wall. Along comes my father and grabs hold of my arm.

"Hussey!" said he, "give me the key quickly, or I will throw you in the pond."

Very speedily I pulled the key out of my pocket, and gave it to him, and was very sad and silent. I saw it to be in vain to say anything to him. I went my way down beside my father's woods, sighing and groaning to God as I went along. As I was a-going, that Scripture came in upon my mind: "Call upon Me and I will answer thee, and shew thee great and mighty things that thou knowest not." Sometimes I would be ready to say in my

heart, "Lord, what mighty things wilt Thou show me?"
So I remained by the woodside crying bitterly. It was a
very dark night.

As any rational body must needs think, these were
hard things for me to meet with. But that word was
blessed to me, "The eyes of the Lord are upon the
righteous, and his ear open to their cry." And another
Scripture as well was a wonderful word, "In all their
afflictions, He was afflicted."

I stayed away so long my brother and sister grew
concerned for me and sent some of their men to father on
some errand, for only the purpose to see whether I was
gone in. They returned with the answer that the old
master was alone, I was not there. Then my brother and
some of the family went about seeking for me, but found
me not. When at last I returned I began to think what to
do, for this was the case—if I would promise my father
never to go to a meeting again, he would let me in. That
I will never do, thought I to myself, not if I have to beg
my bread from door to door. I thought I was so strongly
fixed in this resolution that nothing could move me and
that whatever I met with from my father, I should never
yield. But poor, weak creature that I was, just like Peter,
as you will hear afterwards. This was Saturday night.

When Sabbath day morning came I said to my brother, "Let us call and see father as we go to the meeting." But he said, "No, it will but provoke him." So we went not. As we walked to the meeting my brother talked to me. "Sister," said he, "you are now brought upon the stage to act for Christ and His ways. I would not have you consent to father on his terms." "No, brother," said I, "not if I beg my bread from door to door." I did not think I needed any cautions on that account. As I sat in the meeting my mind was very much harried and troubled, and no wonder, considering my circumstances. In the evening as we came back I again said, "Let us go to my father," and he consented.

We found him in the yard, a-serving the cows. Before we came into the yard my brother warned me again not to consent to my father, or to forsake the ways of God, but I still thought I had no need of his counsel. My brother talked with father very mildly and pleaded with him to be reconciled to me, but he was angry and would not hear him, so I whispered to my brother and bid him go away. "No," said he, "I will not go without you." "I will come presently," was my reply. But as he said afterwards he was afraid to leave me, for fear I should yield, but I thought I could as soon part with my life. So my brother and sister went home, and I remained in the yard talking to my father and pleading with him to let me go in. He had the key of the house in his pocket.

OH, DISMAL NIGHT!

"Father," said I, "I will serve you in anything that lies in me to do for you, as long as you live. And, father, I only want to hear God's Word if you will but let me go to the meeting. You can't answer for my sins or stand before God instead of me." He replied that if I would promise him never to go to a meeting as long as he lived, I could go in and he would treat me the same as his other children, but if not I should never have a farthing. "Father," said I, "my soul is of more worth than that. I dare not make such a promise."

My poor brother's heart ached when he saw that I did not follow him. Father grew very angry and bid me begone and not trouble him, for his mind was made up. "If," said he, "you will promise me never to go to a meeting again, I will give you the key and you shall go in." He kept on holding the key out to me to see if I would promise him. I, as often, refused to yield. At last he got impatient. "Hussey," said he, "what do you say? If you will promise me never to go to a meeting again as long as I live, here is the key; take it and go in. I will never offer it to you again and you shall never come within my door again while I live."

25

So there I stood crying by him in the yard. "What do you say, hussey?," said he. "Will you promise me or no?"

"Well, father, I will promise you that I will never go to a meeting again, as long as you live, without your consent." I never thought what misery I was bringing on myself in so saying. He gave me the key. I unlocked the door and went in. As soon as I was inside, that dreadful Scripture came to my mind: "They that deny Me before men, them will I deny before My Father and the angels that are in heaven," and also that word, "He that forsaketh not father and mother and all that he hath, is not worthy of Me." Oh, thought I! What will become of me now? What have I done this night? I started to run out of the house, but, thought I, that won't help matters. All my comfort was gone. In its room I had nothing but terror and guilt of conscience. Now I saw what all my resolutions came to. This was Sunday night, a black night.

My poor father came in and was very loving to me, and asked me to get him some supper, which I did. He bid me come and eat, but, oh, it was a bitter supper to me. My brother was troubled because I did not come to his house, and wondered why I stayed so long. He feared and guessed what I had done, but to make sure, he sent one of his men on some errand to see if I was in the house. He returned with the answer that I was in the house with the old master and that he was very cheerful. Then was my brother much troubled, for he knew that I had yielded, else father would not have let me in. No tongue can express what a doleful condition I was in. Neither durst I look up to God for mercy. Oh now, I thought, I must hear God's Word no more! What a wretch am I to deny Christ, after He has been so good to me in all my troubles, and now I have turned my back on Him. "Oh, black night," said I. "Oh, dismal night, in which I have denied my dear Saviour." When I had seen my father off to bed, I too went to bed, but it was a sad night to me.

The next morning, which was Monday, came my brother. "Oh, sister," said he, "what have you done? What do you say to that Scripture 'he that denieth Me before men, him will I deny before My Father and the angels that are in heaven'." This was the salutation that he gave me. Oh, thought I, it is this that cuts my heart, but I said little to him, only wept bitterly. Then father came in and John said no more, except "Good morrow, father," and went away. I can't express the misery I was in. I filled every corner of the house with sighs and tears.

I went crying about as if my very heart would have burst with grief and horror. Now and then one blessed promise or another would fall into my mind, such as "Simon, Satan hath desired to have thee, that he may sift thee as wheat, but I have prayed for thee." But the thought which lay uppermost was that I must hear God's Word no more. Now, thought I, if my father could give me thousands of gold, what good would it do me? Thus I went groaning about till I was almost spent. Whenever my father went out I filled the house with dismal cries. Yet I told not my grief to my brother, for I thought he would not pity me. Nor did I ever tell him what I went through at that time. When father came in, then I went out to the barns or outhouses to cry there. As I stood sighing and crying like a poor distracted body and leaning my head against the wall, saying, "Lord, what shall I do? Lord, what shall I do?," those words dropped into my mind, "There shall be made a way for you to escape, that you may be able to bear it." "Lord," said I, "what way shall be made? Will my father be made willing for me to go to meetings?" If it should be so, thought I, what a wretch I had been to deny Christ. Oh, now the pardon of my sins seemed worth a world. Forgiveness of sins was what I cried for, saying, "Lord, pity and pardon, pity and pardon."

At night, as my father and I sat by the fire, he asked me what the matter was, for he had noticed how sorrowful I had been all day. I burst out crying. "Oh, father," said I, "I am so afflicted to think that I have promised you never to go to a meeting again without your consent. And the fears I have, lest you never let me go again." He wept like a child. "Well, don't let that trouble you," said he, "we shall not disagree."

At this I was a little comforted. "Pray, father," said I, "forgive me where I have been undutiful to you, or disobedient in anything." So he sat there weeping and told me how troubled he was for me that night when he shut me out, and could not sleep; but that he thought I had gone to my brother's house. It was my riding behind John Bunyan which vexed him. That enemy in the town had incensed him against Mr. Bunyan. Some time ago, my father had heard him preach and heard him with a broken heart. For when I was first awakened he was mightily concerned to see me in such distress about my soul, and said to neighbours who came to the house, "I think my daughter will go mad; she scarcely eats, drinks or sleeps, yet I have lived these three score years and scarcely ever thought of my soul." After that he would pray to God just as I did and go to meetings and heard God's Word with tears, until that evil-minded man in the town turned him against the meetings. I have stood and heard him say to my father, "Have you lived all these years to be led away by them?," even quoting (wrongly) that Scripture: "These are they that lead silly women captive and for a pretence make long prayers." So he kept on until he had set him against me and the meetings and would advise him not to let me go.

This was Monday night, but notwithstanding what father had said, I was still full of sorrow and guilt of conscience, and spent much time that night in praying for pardon of my sin and that God would keep me by His grace for time to come. I saw then what all my strong resolutions came to.

The next day came, which was Tuesday, in which I still remained very sorrowful, weeping and crying bitterly, but as I remember, God lifted me up before night. I was able to believe my sins were forgiven. Many good words came into my heart which I have forgotten. I then began to look back with comfort to Friday night in the barn, and to think of that blessed word "beloved," and I did believe that Jesus Christ was the same yesterday, to-day, and forever. All that day I spent in praying to God in corners, except when I did my work about the house, and got father his dinner. And he ate as good a dinner as ever I saw him eat.

Well, night came on, which indeed was a very dismal night to me, and had not the Lord stood by me and strengthened me, I had certainly sunk down under all that happened. But God was faithful; He did not let me be tempted more than I was able to bear. Towards night that Scripture often ran in my mind: "In six troubles I will be with thee, and in seven I will not leave thee."

In the evening my father said, "It is a very cold night; we will not sit up too long to-night." When the nights were long he would sometimes sit up with me, a candle burning while I sat aspinning or at other work, but this time he said it was so cold he would have his supper and go to bed. After supper, as he sat by the fire, he took a pipe of tobacco. When he had finished he bid me to take up the coals and warm his bed; which I did. As I pulled the covers over him, these words ran through my mind: "The end is come, the end is come, the time draweth near." I could not tell what to make of them, for they were very dark to me. So I went out of his room into the kitchen.

THE END IS COME!

Now the chamber where my father lay had two beds. It was a lower room, so I could hear my father when he was asleep as I sat by the fire in the next room; for he used to snore so in his sleep that one might hear him all over the house. When I heard him snore I often took liberty to stay up longer and improve the time. That night he slept very soundly, and although he had told me to make haste to bed, I did not do so but spent some time in prayer. I found my heart wonderfully drawn out to ask for several things in a more earnest manner than I had felt for a long time. One thing for which I pleaded with God was that he would show mercy to my dear father and save his soul. I could not tell when to stop beseeching God for this thing, yet that word still ran through my mind: "The end is come, the end is come, the time draweth near. The set time is come." But not one thought had I that it had respect to father's death. Another thing I was crying to the Lord for was, that He would be pleased to stand by me and be with me in whatever I had to meet with in this world, never dreaming what I should meet with during that very night and the week following. So it was that I prayed as if I had known what was coming upon me—which, of course, I did not.

After a long time spent in this way I went to bed. When I came into the room my father was still asleep, which I was glad of, for if he happened to hear me come to bed after I had sat up for a long time, he would chide me for staying up so late. So I got into bed with a thankful heart. After a time I fell asleep. But it was not long, I suppose, before I heard a very doleful noise. At first, not being quite awake, I thought the noise was in the yard. At last it wakened me more and more and I perceived it came from my father. On hearing him make such a dreadful noise I started up in bed.

"Father!" said I. "Are you not well?" "No," he replied. "How long have you not been well, pray?" "I was struck," said he, "with a pain at my heart in my sleep. I shall die immediately."

I jumped out of bed, slipped on my petticoats and shoes, lit a candle, and ran to his bedside. He sat upright in his bed calling out to God for mercy. "Lord," cried he, "have mercy on me. I am a poor miserable sinner. Lord Jesus, wash me in Thy precious blood."

I stood by him, trembling to hear him in such distress of soul for Christ and to see him look so pale in the face. Then I knelt down by his bedside and prayed for him out loud as well as I could. He joined with me, oh, so earnestly! When I had done this, which was more than I had ever done with him before, I said to him, "Father, I must go and call someone; I dare not stay with you alone." For there was nobody with us nor was there any house near.

"You shall not go out at this time of night," said he. "Don't be afraid over me." But he still made the house ring with cries for mercy. Then he said he would get up and put some clothes on. I ran out and made up a good fire, in readiness for when he came out of the bedroom. All the while he called and prayed for mercy and cried out of a pain at his heart. This, thought I, is a cold that has settled about his heart for want of taking hot things when he had shut me out, and had no one to do anything for him. So I ran and made him a hot drink, hoping he might be better.

"Oh," cried he, "I want mercy for my soul. Oh, Lord, show mercy to me, I am a great sinner. Oh, Lord Jesus, if Thou dost not show mercy to me now, I am undone for ever."

"Father," said I, "there is mercy in Jesus Christ for sinners. Lord help you to lay hold of it."

"Oh," said he, "I have been against you for seeking after Jesus Christ; the Lord forgive me, and lay not that sin to my charge."

When I had made him something hot, I prayed him to drink some of it. He drank a little and then strained to vomit, but did not. So I ran to him and held his head as he sat by the fire. He went black in the face as if he was dying and as I stood by him, holding his head, he leant against me with all his weight. This was a very frightful thing to me indeed! If I leave him, thought I, he will fall on the fire, and if I stand by him,

he will die in my arms, and not a soul to help me! "Oh," I cried out, "Lord, help me, what shall I do?" Those words darted into my mind, "Fear not, I am with thee; be not dismayed, I am thy God, I will help thee, I will uphold thee."

After a little while it pleased God that my father should revive and come to himself. Again he cried out for mercy. "Lord, have mercy upon me. I am a sinful man; Lord, spare me one week more, one day more." These were piercing words to me. So, after sitting by the fire for a while, he came quite round; for he had, I think, swooned away for a time.

"Give me the candle," said he, "I will go to the bedroom." He took the candle and went into the chamber. I saw him stagger as he stepped over the threshold. I then made the fire up again ready for when he came out. When I had done that I went immediately into his room. As soon as I came through the doorway I saw him lying on the ground and ran to him screaming and crying.

"Father! Father!" I cried, and put my hands under his arms, pulling and pulling in a vain attempt to lift him up. So I stood tugging at him and crying till my strength was gone, first at one arm, then at the other. Some folks said afterwards that my dream of the apple tree did signify something of this. There I stood, lifting and crying, until I was almost spent. I could perceive no life in him. Now, I was in a strait indeed! When I saw I could not possibly lift him up, I left him and ran through the house crying like the poor afflicted creature that I was.

I then unlocked the door to go and call my brother. Now, it was the dead time of the night and no other house near. As I ran through the door the thought gripped me that there were rogues hiding behind it, ready to knock me on the head, at which I was greatly afraid; but when I thought how my poor father lay dead in the house I saw that I was now surrounded with trouble, so I opened the door and rushed out much affrighted. It had snowed abundantly that night. It lay very deep. I had no stockings on and the snow got into my shoes so that I could not run quickly. When I got to the stile that was in our yard, I stood on it crying and calling to my brother. At last God helped me to realize that it was impossible to hear me from that distance, so I got over the stile. The snow-water made my shoes come off, but I ran as fast as I could towards my brother's house. As I ran I got the fear that robbers were after me to kill me, but as I hastily looked behind me, that verse came to me: "The angel of the Lord encampeth round about them that fear Him."

FATHER IS DEAD!

So, coming to my brother's house, I stood crying out in a doleful manner under his chamber window, surprising and frightening his whole family, they being in their midnight sleep. My brother was so alarmed he did not recognize my voice. He jumped out of bed, put his head out of the window, crying, "Who are you? What is the matter?" "Oh, brother," said I, "Father is dead! Come away quickly." At that he withdrew from the window and I heard him say, "Oh, wife, it is my poor sister. She says father is dead."

Then my brother called up his men, but they were so scared they could hardly put on their clothes, and when they came out of doors they seemed, for a moment, as if they did not know me. Eventually, John and two or three of his men set off at a run and got to our house before me. They found my father had risen from the ground and was laid on the bed. My brother spoke to him and stood crying over him, but father could say no more than one or two words. When I came in, they would not let me come to the bed, for they said he was just departing. Oh, dismal night! Indeed, as I said, had not the Lord been good to me I should have been frightened out of my wits.

One of my brother's men came to me presently and told me that father was gone. I had, in spite of all my grief, some hopes that he had gone to heaven. As I sat there crying, and thinking what a great change death had made upon poor father, who went well to bed and by midnight was in eternity, I said in my heart, "Lord, give me one sign more that I shall go to heaven when death shall make this great change in me." While I was saying this, some words of Scripture suddenly came into my mind: "The ransomed of the Lord shall return, and come with singing to Zion, and everlasting joy shall be upon their heads. They shall obtain joy and gladness; and sorrow and sighing shall fly away." This gave me such a vivid sense of the joys of the saints that I longed to go to heaven. "They are singing," thought I. "But I am sorrowing, yet it is a great mercy that I have any hope of going there."

Soon after my brother came, he sent some of his men to call the neighbours. Among the rest came Mr. Freery and his son. Immediately upon entering the house, Mr. Freery asked if father was departed. Somebody told him that he had. "It is no more than I expected," was his reply. Now, no one took any notice of those words until afterwards. Then some women came in, who saw me sitting there without my stockings and scarcely any clothes on me, and sympathized with me in my sad state and all the terrifying things which I had met with that night.

It was Tuesday night that father died, and I now remembered the verse of Scripture which came to me in the barn on the previous Friday. "Beloved, think it not strange concerning the fiery trials which are to try you." "I have had fiery trials since Friday night indeed," said I to myself, little thinking I had as bad, or worse, still to come.

YOUR SISTER POISONED HIM!

Well, on that same Tuesday there was a fair at Baldock; and the priest, Mr. Lane, who saw Mr. Bunyan and me on horseback at Gamlingay was at the fair. He spread it about that he had seen me behind Mr. Bunyan riding to Gamlingay and that when we came to the town's end he saw us misbehaving ourselves together. This report, as I heard later, quickly spread from one end of the fair to the other.

On the next day after the fair, Wednesday morning, while my poor father was lying dead in the house, someone came and told me of the evil report there was of me at Baldock Fair; but that verse helped me which says, "Blessed are ye when men shall revile you, and say all manner of evil of you falsely, for My name's sake."

Then my brother came over again and we arranged that father should be buried on Thursday evening. He ordered the wine and all things necessary to be delivered Thursday morning. We also sent off invitations to all our friends and relations for several miles round about us to come on Thursday. When all this was done, Mr. Freery sent for my brother to come to his house. So, on the Wednesday night, my brother went and Mr. Freery invited him into the parlour to speak with him privately. "I have a mind to speak with you," said he. "Do you think your father died a natural death?"

My brother was amazed to hear him ask such a question. "I know he died a natural death," answered he.

"I believe he did not," replied Mr. Freery. "Twice to-day I got my horse out of the stable, intending to fetch Mr. Halfhead of Potton, the Doctor; but on thinking it over, I decided to leave it to you. You are an officer of the town. Therefore, see you do your duty."

"How do you think he did die," said my brother, "if he came not by his end in a natural way?"

"I believe your sister poisoned him."

"I hope," replied my brother, "that we shall satisfy you to the contrary."

Well, my brother came home with a heavy heart, for he did not know but what I might lose my life, and he was very troubled to think what I had yet to meet with. First, he called my sister upstairs and told her about it, which caused great distress in them both. There was a good man in the town at Sister Prudon's house, so they sent for him and told him of this thing. The three of them went into an upper room and spread it before the Lord. My brother then asked the other two whether he had better come across to our farm that night and tell me. "No," said they, "let her have this night in quiet."

HAVE THE BODY OPENED!

Next morning early, my brother came with a very sad countenance and called me upstairs. "Sister," said he, "I must speak with you." I went up with him into the chamber, and as soon as we were up, he fell a-weeping.

"Oh, sister," said he. "Pray God may help you, for you are like to meet with hard things."

"Hard things?," said I. "What, worse than I have met with already?"

"Yes, worse than anything you have met with yet."

Then he told me how our neighbour, Mr. Freery, accused me of father's death, saying that I had poisoned him. At the first hearing of this my heart sank and indeed it was a sad surprise, but I quickly made reply. "Oh, brother, blessed be God for a clear conscience." Yet, as anyone must need agree, these were hard things for one as young as I to meet with.

"I must send," said my brother, "to Potton for Mr. Halfhead, who is both a doctor and a surgeon." We also had to send a message to all those we had invited to the funeral, desiring them not to come until they heard further from us. This made many people in the town, and other towns round about, wonder what the matter was, especially as they knew my father was not in debt.

When Mr. Halfhead came we told him how things were, that someone in the town did think that I had poisoned my father. He questioned me as to how my father was before he went to bed, and what supper he ate. I told him everything he asked me, and he seemed to be very sorry for me. After he had viewed the corpse he called on Mr. Freery and told him he wondered how he could entertain such thoughts about me. His reply to Mr. Halfhead was that he believed his suspicions to be the truth.

When Mr. Halfhead saw no arguments would convince Mr. Freery, he came back to us and said we must have a coroner and a jury. "Sir," said I, "I pray you to cut my father open. As my innocency is known to God, so I would have it known to men."

"No," replied he. "There is no need to have the body opened."

We then asked him to come the next day to meet the coroner and jury. He said he would. Now had I a fresh work in front of me, and betook myself to prayer, asking God for help, that He would please to appear for me in this fiery trial, for I saw my very life was at stake, and the good name of all godly folk too. Many prayers and tears I poured out to God, and a sweet cordial He sent to comfort me. Oh, it was a blessed promise indeed (and, blessed be God, He also made good His word)! "No weapon that is formed against thee shall prosper, and every tongue that shall rise up in judgment against thee, thou shalt condemn." Also another verse kept coming into my mind: "As many as are incensed against thee shall be ashamed."

Next morning, which was Friday, my brother sent for the coroner and jury to come that day. Mr. Freery, hearing that they had been sent for, asked my brother to go to his house, which he did. "I hear you have sent for the coroner," said Mr. Freery.

"Yes," replied my brother.

"I would wish," said the other, "that you should meet the coroner at Biggleswade and settle the matter there. Do not let him come here, for it will be found to be petty treason and your sister will be burned."

"We are not afraid," replied my brother. "We are not afraid to let the coroner come here."

My brother then came and told me what Mr. Freery said.

HOW SHALL I ENDURE BURNING?

"Brother," said I, "I will have the coroner come through here, even if it costs me all that father left me, for if we do not, then Mr. Freery and all the world would say I am guilty indeed!" Although I spoke thus, I saw that my life was at stake, for I did not know how far God would allow Mr. Freery and the devil to go. It also troubled me to realize that if I suffered, another, just as innocent, must suffer too. Mr. Freery said I had plotted against my father, and that John Bunyan advised me to poison him when I rode behind him to Gamlingay. He said we did then agree to do it. Nay, if I remember rightly, it was said that Mr. Bunyan gave me the stuff to do it with! But the Lord knew to the contrary, that neither he nor I was guilty of that wickedness, in thought, word, or deed. Yet, although I knew myself clear, I could see I was in sore straits and surrounded by trouble. Carnal reasoning got in. "Suppose God should allow my enemies to prevail and take away my life?," thought I. "How shall I endure burning?" Oh, this made my heart beat at a great rate, but blessed be God I was innocent in thought, word, and deed. Still the thoughts of burning would sometimes shake me all to pieces, and sometimes I thought of that Scripture which had been so often in my mind before father died: "When thou goest through the fire, I will be with thee, and through the waters, they shall not overflow thee." Then I would think thus: "Lord, Thou knowest I am innocent, therefore, if it shall please Thee to let them take away my life, yet Thou wilt be with me. Thou hast been with me through all my straits, and surely Thou wilt not leave me now in the greatest of all." Arguing thus from the experience of God's goodness to me in previous times of trial, I was able to believe that even if I did burn at a stake, the Lord would give me His presence. So I was made, in a solemn manner, I hope, to resign myself up to God, to be at His disposal, for life or death. But still I was troubled for the honour of God's name which I thought must be injured whichever way it went with me; for there would doubtless be many who would believe me guilty whatever the jury might say. But in the end I realized I must leave the matter with God, who has the hearts of all men in His hand.

The coroner was not due to come until the afternoon, so in the morning of the same day some of the friends from Gamlingay came to me and spent some time in prayer that God would graciously appear for me, and for the glory of His own name. After they had finished I got into a corner by myself, for I had a great mind to be with God alone, a thing which I usually found to be of great help to me. Also I desired particularly to ask for His presence that day, so that I might not have a dejected countenance, nor be of a daunted spirit in front of them. For I could see that to be brought before a company of men, and accused of murdering my father, would be so fearful a thing that even though I knew myself to be innocent, yet I should be ready to faint with shame, unless God should be with me. "If they see me look daunted and dejected," thought I, "they will think I am guilty." So I begged of the Lord that He would carry me up above the fear of men, devils, and death itself, and that He would give me faith and courage to look my accusers boldly in the face, so that when they saw me with my head held high they should by my very expression be convinced of my innocence.

As I was earnestly praying, a Scripture darted into my mind: "The righteous shall hold on their way, and they that have clean hands shall grow stronger and stronger." "Oh, Lord," I exclaimed, "Thou knowest my hands and my heart are clean in this matter." The words seemed so exactly suitable that I could scarce have had the like—but the Lord was as good as His word, every little bit of it, ere the sun went down.

Presently word was brought that the jury had come to my brother's house. When they had stabled their horses and got all in readiness, they walked across to our house to view the corpse. I, with some neighbours, were by the fire and as the jurymen passed through the house into the room where my father was laid out, some of them came and took me by the hand with tears running down their cheeks, and said to me, "Pray God be thy comfort, for thou art as innocent as we are." So one and another spoke to me in this way, and truly I looked on this as a mercy to me, to see them so convinced of my innocence.

When the coroner had seen my father's body, he came into the room and stood and warmed himself by the fire. He stared at me with a steadfast look and said,

"Are you the daughter of this man now deceased?"

"Yes, Sir," said I.

"Are you she that was in the house alone with him when he died?"

"Yes, Sir, I am she."

He then shook his head in a way which made me think he had evil thoughts of me and not good.

After this they all went back to my brother's house again, and when they had dined and were ready to sit, my brother sent for me. As I was going, my heart went out to God to stand by me. Such words as these passed through my mind: "Thou shalt not return again ashamed." Before I came to the house I was so wonderfully borne up in my spirits, even beyond what I asked or thought was possible, that truly, as it says in the Song of Songs, "My soul was like the chariots of Amminadab."

As soon as I arrived Mr. Freery was sent for, but he did not come. So my brother sent for him again. At last he came and the inquest was begun.

The coroner called the witnesses, my brother's men that were with my father when he died, and gave them the oath. Likewise, Mr. Freery was also sworn "to speak the truth and nothing but the truth." As far as I remember, my brother's men were examined first. They answered all the coroner asked them, which was whether they were there before my father died, to which they answered "Yes," and how long he lived after they came, and what words they heard him speak. The coroner finished with them very quickly. Then he called Mr. Freery.

"Come," said he, "you are the cause of our coming together. We would know what you have to say as to this maid murdering her father, and what grounds you have for accusing her?"

Mr. Freery made such a strange preamble that nobody knew what to make of it, talking of the quarrel there was between my father and I, and of my being shut out of doors, and of father dying two nights after I came in.

There I stood in the parlour among them all with my heart so full of comfort as ever it could hold; I had got above the fear of men or devils.

"This is nothing to do with the matter in hand!" said the coroner. "What have you to bring against this maid?"

But Mr. Freery said little or nothing which was to the purpose. The coroner grew angry with the contrary answers he gave to the questions he asked him. I have forgotten his pitiful answers. At last the coroner got very angry and told him to stand down if that was all he could say.

The coroner called me, "Come, sweetheart," said he, "tell us where you were the night your father shut you out?"

Now the man that went to Bedford to fetch the coroner had told him how all things were as they rode along together.

"Sir," said I, "I was in the barn all night."

"And wast thou there alone all night?"

"Yes, Sir, I had nobody with me."

So he shook his head. "And where did you go next morning?"

"Sir," said I, "I stayed in the yard until about nine or ten o'clock trying to persuade him to let me go in; but he would not." The coroner seemed concerned at hearing this. He asked me where I spent that day.

"Sir, I went to my brother's house."

"And where were you that night?"

I told him I slept at my brother's house as my brother's men had said in their evidence.

He asked me when my father let me in to his house.

I told him the Sabbath day night.

He asked me if he was well, and how long it was after I came in that he died.

"Sir," said I, "it was Sabbath night when I went in, and he died the next Tuesday night."

"Was he well on that day?"

"Yes, Sir. He was as well as ever I saw him in my life, and ate as good a dinner as ever I saw him eat."

He asked me what he ate at supper.

So I told him.

He asked me in what manner he was taken ill, and what time.

"Sir," said I, "the manner of his being taken ill was in his sleep, with a pain at his heart as he told me afterwards. As to the time, it was a little before midnight. I, being in the same room, heard him groan. I made haste to get out of bed, lit a candle and went to him. He sat upright in his bed, crying out of a pain at his heart and that he was going to die immediately. I was so badly frightened, I could scarcely put any clothes on. Then he said he would get up, so I made the fire up and he sat by it. I ran and got him something hot. He drank a little of it and then strained as if he were going to be sick. I ran to hold his head and he swooned away. I could not leave him to call for anybody. If I had he would have dropped into the fire, for he leant against me with all his weight."

"Was there no one in the house with you?"

"No, Sir," said I, "nobody with me but God."

So he shook his head.

"When my father came to himself he said he wanted to go to his room. I followed soon afterwards and he lay all along on the ground. I ran screaming to him and lifted at him, but I could not lift him, so I left him, and ran in a frightful state to my brother's house."

The man that went for the coroner had told him how I frightened the family.

"Sweetheart," said the coroner, "I have no more to say to thee."

Next he spoke to the jury. When they had given their verdict and all was done, he turned to Mr. Freery.

"You that have defamed this maid in this manner, you must needs make it your business now to repair her reputation again. You have taken away her good name from her and you would have taken away her life, if you could. She met with enough trouble, I think, in being in the house alone that night when her father died. You need not have added this to her affliction and sorrow. If you should give her five hundred pounds it would not make amends to her."

The coroner came to me and took me by the hand. "Come, sweetheart," said he, "do not be daunted, God will take care of thee, and provide you a husband, notwithstanding the malice of this man. Bless God for this deliverance. Never fear, He will take care of thee, but I must confess these are hard things for one so young as thou art to meet with."

I had a mind to speak to the coroner and jury before they went away. "Sir," said I, "if you are not all satisfied I am freely willing that my father should be opened. As my innocence is known to God, so I would have it known to you. I am not afraid for my life."

"No," said he. "We are well satisfied of thy innocence; there is no need to have him opened. But," said he, "bless God that the malice of this man broke out before thy father was buried."

The room where we were was very full of people, and it seems great observation was made of my face, as I heard afterwards. Some gentlemen that sat upon the jury said they would never forget with what a cheerful countenance I stood before them all. They said I did not look like one who was guilty. I know not how I looked, but I know my heart was full of peace and comfort. All the members of the jury were very concerned for me. It was noticed that many of them sat with wet eyes while the coroner was questioning me. Indeed, I had good cause to thank God that they were convinced of my innocence. I heard that for twelve months afterwards, they would speak of me with tears.

We now sent out invitations again to all our friends to come to my father's funeral on Saturday night. Now, thought I, surely my troubles and trials connected with that matter will all be at an end. I thought Mr. Freery had now vented all his spite, but, no, he was resolved to have yet another pull with me. Seeing he was prevented from taking away my life, he did attempt to take away what my father left me. He sent for my brother-in-law, who had married my sister, and told him how things were left in my father's will, and that his wife was cut off with but a shilling. He told my brother-in-law he could put him in the way to get at least a part of what my father had left to me. My brother-in-law was pleased to hear this.

Now, my father's will was made three years before he died, and Mr. Freery made it. It was he who persuaded my father to give me more than my sister. He did this for a particular reason he then had, but afterwards, when I began to go to meetings, he turned against me. For all I knew, the will could have been altered, but, however, it was not. So the next thing I had to put up with was that I must either give up a part of what father had left me to my brother-in-law or else he would sue me. This was a fresh trouble, for I was threatened at a great rate. Mr. Freery said, "Hang her, and do not let her get away with so much more than your wife." And to law they would have gone immediately unless I had given my brother sixty pounds for peace and quietness.

One great mercy the Lord was pleased to add to all the rest. He kept hatred for this man out of my heart, and I was able to pray to God for him in secret, so that I can say I longed for salvation for his soul and begged forgiveness for what he had done against me.

About a month after father was buried, a fresh rumour was raised about me. It was hotly reported at Biggleswade that I had now confessed that I had poisoned my father, and that I was quite distracted. I heard that whole groups of people would get together to discuss this news, and that while some would say, "But is it true?" there were others who did not hesitate to say, "Yes, it is true enough."

"Well," thought I, "if it pleases God to spare me, I will go next market day to let them see that I am not distracted." I was troubled to think the name of God might suffer. When Wednesday morning came I made me ready to go to Biggleswade. It was very cold with frost and snow, but I could not be contented without going. The Lord was wonderfully good that morning, and that Scripture ran strongly in my mind as I went to the market: "Blessed are ye, when men shall revile you, and say all manner of evil against you falsely for My name's sake; rejoice and be exceeding glad, for great is your reward in heaven." Also those words: "As many as are incensed against thee shall be ashamed." When I got there, I went to Sister Edwards' to rest, and then, when it was full market, I went out to show myself among them. As soon as I appeared, most of the people forgot the business they were about at that particular moment, and I think I may say almost every eye was fixed on me. Here I could see half a dozen standing together whispering and pointing; there I could see another group talking and staring. I walked through and through the market. "If there were a thousand more of you," thought I, "I could lift up my head before you all," for I was very well in my soul that day.

A large number came up to me and said, "Well, we can see you are not out of your mind." I saw some crying, while others laughed. "Oh," thought I, "mock on; for there is a day coming which will make everything clear." That was a wonderful Scripture to me: "He will bring forth thy righteousness as the light and thy brightness shall be as the noonday."

Thus I have told you of the good and evil things I met with in those days. I wish I was as well in my soul now as I was then.

Agnes Beaumont's cottage at Edworth
24. 3. '62 LfL

EPILOGUE

So Agnes ends her simple tale, at the supreme moment of her life. Let the curtain fall there. She had been intensely anxious (even though she knew she was innocent) lest through some miscarriage of justice she should be found guilty, and thus the name of God be dishonoured. She was brought to learn the valuable lesson that it is what we are before God that matters, and, with the other persecuted Puritans, to look far beyond fallible human justice to the divine Court of Law.

It only remains to add a few brief notes for those whose interest in this persecuted servant of God would cause them to be disappointed if they did not know anything of her subsequent history. Mr. Freery, the villainous family lawyer, remained unrelenting in his persecution. Far from making amends as the coroner had commanded, he spread false tales about her; one, that she was married to John Bunyan, and another that, when during a hot summer a house in Edworth caught fire, it was Agnes who had set it alight.

"God," the coroner had said, "will provide thee a husband." He spake better than he knew, for God provided her with two. With her first husband, of whose name we have no record, she lived in a farmhouse at Blunham, which still stands. With her second husband, Mr. Story, a man of considerable substance and great seriousness, she lived at Highgate until her death in her sixty-ninth year on November 28th, 1720. Her body, in compliance with her last wish, was brought to Hitchin, where in the burial-ground of the Baptist Church she might be laid to earth beside her fellow members and close to John Wilson, her lifelong friend and pastor.

AGNES BEAUMONT
OF EDWORTH, BEDFORDSHIRE
(Afterwards Mrs STORY)
Became a member of the Church at Bedford
under the pastoral Care of the
Revd JOHN BUNYAN, Oct 31st 1672
Died at HIGHGATE. NOV. 28th 1720
Aged 68 Years
And being brougt to HITCHIN
by her own desire
was interred in the adjoining Ground

The Heritage Set for Girls

If your family enjoyed <u>Behind Mr. Bunyan</u>, you – especially your girls – are certain to enjoy the other volumes in this rare, 19th century set!

The Dairyman's Daughter	$5.00
I Have A Soul	$4.00
The Little Girls' Treasury	$6.50
First Impressions of God	$5.00
Patty's Curiosity	$4.00
The Young Cottager	$5.00
Grace Raymond	$4.00
Little Mary	$5.00

for further reading about John Bunyan, and family

<u>Mary Bunyan: Blind Daughter of John Bunyan</u>

You will never read a more deeply moving story than this, of the Bunyan's home life as John languished in prison for his faith and preaching. Told from the perspective of their blind daughter Mary and how her faith grows during difficult times.　(528 pages, paperback)　**$11.50**

<u>The Fear of God</u> by John Bunyan

This is the beginning of wisdom! (Prov. 1:7). Bunyan shows us the reasons to fear God, what true fear of God is, its effects on our lives, the privileges of those who fear God, and more. Includes a study guide, for personal or group study.
(220 pages) **$15.00** hardcover / **$7.00** paperback

Continued, next page ~ ~ ~

The Holy War by John Bunyan
In the city of Mansoul, a fierce battle rages for control of the life! Who will conquer: Diabolus or Emmanuel? And what can the residents do to resist the attacks of the evil one? Your soul is under attack from the forces of evil. Through this powerful allegory, learn how Christ conquers, and how you can grow through spiritual warfare. (192 pages, paperback) **$9.50**

The Pilgrim's Progress by John Bunyan
The most sold and read book in the history of the English language other than the Bible. A vividly picturesque story of a journey from this world of sin to the world to come, full of remarkable insights into the struggles and temptations which accompany Christian living. (375 pages, paperback) **$5.50**

Grace Abounding to the Chief of Sinners
by John Bunyan   A spiritual classic (originally publ. 1666) and one of the most popular of Puritan writings. Bunyan traces his spiritual pilgrimage from his youth through several crises, to his conversion, telling of many trials, temptations and sorrows, until he comes to rely solely on Christ for his every need.   (hardcover, 159 pages) **$13.00**

Dangerous Journey (abridged Pilgrim's Progress)
With beautiful color paintings on every page, this artful book has long been a favorite introductory version of Pilgrim's Progress, for those parents wanting to offer their children a first "taste" of Bunyan's timeless classic.
(illustrated, oversized hardcover, 126 pages) **$19.50**

Continued, next page ~ ~ ~

The Complete Works of John Bunyan
These three, high-quality volumes are the only
available edition of Bunyan's complete works.
Includes all works mentioned above and over 20
more sermons and treatises.   **$115.00 / set**
(3 hardcover folio volumes, 2400 pages)

Prayer by John Bunyan
Two sections, "Praying in the Spirit" and "The
Throne of Grace", filled with rich instruction on
both how to pray and encouraging us to develop
habits of joyfully and boldly coming into the
presence of God in prayer.
(paperback, 172 pages)   **$6.50**

All Loves Excelling by John Bunyan
Originally titled "The Saint's Knowledge of Christ's
Love", this exposition of Ephesians 3:18-19 speaks
of Christ's love as an attempt to "describe the
inexpressible", "desire the incomparable", and
"obtain the unsurpassable."   Among the most
glorious of Puritan writings of all.
(paperback, 129 pages)   **$6.50**

For any of these titles, or our catalogue, contact us at:

Grace & Truth Books

3406 Summit Boulevard
Sand Springs, Oklahoma   74063
Phone: 918 245 1500

www.graceandtruthbooks.com
Email: GTBooksOrders@cs.com

> "The goal of our instruction is love from a pure heart
> and a good conscience and a sincere faith."
> 1 Timothy 1:5